ALICE IN WONDERLAND

HARRY N. ABRAMS, INC., PUBLISHERS, NEW YORK

Library of Congress Cataloging-in-Publication Data

Carroll, Lewis, 1832–1898
Alice in Wonderland

Summary: A little girl falls down a rabbit hole and
discovers a world of nonsensical and amusing characters.
Features twenty-four reproductions of glass slides
originally used in the mid-1880's.
[1. Fantasy] I. Sibley, Brian. II. Title.
PR4611.A7 1987   823′.8 [Fic]   87–15289
ISBN 0–8109–1872–2

Introduction copyright © 1988 Brian Sibley
Text and illustrations copyright © 1988 Justin Knowles Ltd

A Times Mirror Company

Produced by the Justin Knowles Publishing Group
Exeter, U.K.

Designed by Peter Wrigley

Printed and bound in Italy

INTRODUCTION

Alice was beginning to get very tired of sitting by her sister on the bank, and of having nothing to do: once or twice she had peeped into the book her sister was reading, but it had no pictures or conversations in it, "and what is the use of a book," thought Alice, "without pictures or conversations?"

Alice would have liked *this* book: it's full up with pictures and conversations!

The pictures—which have never been seen in a book before—are taken from a set of Victorian Magic Lantern slides; and the conversations are based on those in Lewis Carroll's famous book, *Alice's Adventures in Wonderland.*

The tale of how Alice fell down a rabbit hole and found herself among the curious creatures of Wonderland has been read by millions of children all over the world, but it began as a story told to three very special children on a hot summer's day, more than 125 years ago.

It was July 4, 1862, and the Reverend Charles Lutwidge Dodgson, a thirty-year-old mathematics don at Christ Church, Oxford, had organized an afternoon on the river Thames for his young friends Lorina, Edith, and Alice, daughters of H.G. Liddell, the Dean of Christ Church. A fellow don, the Reverend Robinson Duckworth, was also invited to join the party and help with the rowing.

Although Charles Dodgson was rather shy with adults, he found it very easy to get on with children, probably because he had grown up in a family of seven sisters and three brothers and, over the years, he made many child friends whom he would entertain with stories, poems, games, and puzzles.

The friendship with the Liddell children and, in particular, the pretty, dark-haired Alice, began when Dodgson, who was an excellent amateur photographer, had visited the Deanery in 1857 to take some photographs.

The photographic session led to many more meetings, and to outings such as the river trip in July, 1862.

Writing in his diary that day, Dodgson didn't record quite how remarkable an afternoon it had been: "I made an expedition up the river to Godstow with the three Liddells; we had tea on the bank there, and did not reach Christ Church till half-past eight."

Years later, he was to write of that "golden afternoon" that he could still "call it up almost as clearly as if it were yesterday—the cloudless blue above, the watery mirror below, the boat drifting idly on its way, the tinkle of drops that fell from the oars, as they waved so sleepily to and fro, and (the one bright gleam of life in all the slumberous scene) the three eager faces, hungry for news of fairyland...."

Dodgson's young friends asked for a story. Mr. Dodgson was good at telling stories and making up nonsense rhymes (some of which he had published under the pen name "Lewis Carroll"). The tale he told that day was just another of many he had invented over the years, except that everyone on the trip appreciated that this one was especially good.

All of them were included in the story: Dodgson (who sometimes stuttered his name as "Do-Do-Dodgson") was the Dodo, Duckworth was the Duck, and Lorina and Edith were the Lory and the Eaglet. Of course, the central character was a little girl named Alice.

When they got back to Christ Church that evening, Alice asked Mr. Dodgson to write the story down for her and this he did, lettering each page with great care, adding curious illustrations, and calling it *Alice's Adventures Under Ground.*

At the suggestion of various friends who read the manuscript, Dodgson decided to rewrite the story for publication. In doing so, he added two new episodes in which Alice visited the Duchess and went to A Mad Tea Party—and decided to give the book a new title, since he thought *Alice's Adventures Under Ground* sounded "too much like a lesson book about mines." After considering a number of possibilities, such as *Alice's Hour in Elf-land, Alice Among the Elves* (or *Goblins*), *Alice's Golden Hour,* and *Alice's Doings in Elf-land*—all of which indicate that he thought of his story as a fairytale—Dodgson finally settled on *Alice's Adventures in Wonderland.* Today, however, it is popularly referred to simply as *Alice in Wonderland.*

Realizing that the drawings he had made for the manuscript were not good enough for publication, Dodgson commissioned John Tenniel to illustrate the book. Tenniel was a distinguished artist who, as well as drawing for the humorous magazine *Punch,* had illustrated several books, including an edition of Aesop's Fables, which contained even more animals than were found in Wonderland.

Alice's Adventures in Wonderland was published in 1865 and became a huge success, not least because Tenniel's pictures brought Dodgson's characters vividly to life. For many years Tenniel's conception of Alice—whom he drew as a blonde—the White Rabbit, the Cheshire Cat, the Hatter, and the rest of the company remained unchallenged; even now, despite the efforts of the hundreds of artists who have since illustrated the book, they seem the authoritative interpretation.

Tenniel's drawings later inspired the lively, colorful illustrations in this book, which were originally designed as Magic Lantern slides.

The invention of the Magic Lantern is credited to Athanasius Kircher, a Jesuit priest who described the machine in the second edition of his book, *Ars Magna Lucis et Umbrae* (Great Art of Light and Shadow) published in 1671, although Magic Lanterns were known earlier and Samuel Pepys seems to have owned a similar device in 1666. But it was the Victorians who popularized the Magic Lantern. By burning a mixture of oxygen and hydrogen, they produced a dazzlingly brilliant light (known as "limelight") with which they projected illustrations for public lectures and for home entertainment.

Initially, lantern slides were hand-drawn and painted onto the glass; but from around 1870, the Chromolithographic slide was introduced with color illustrations applied to the glass by transfer and then protected by a second piece of glass.

The Magic Lantern became so popular that smaller versions, illuminated with an oil lamp, were introduced to provide entertainment in the home, especially for the children for whom many sets of slides were made featuring well known fairy tales.

Alice was an obvious subject for a set of lantern slides and Dodgson's publishers, Macmillan & Company, were first approached for permission to use the story and its illustrations in 1876.

The twenty-four slides shown here were produced by Primus, the London photographic company of William Butcher, and sold in three boxed sets of eight slides, price 2/—(about fifty cents). The original colourist is unknown but was probably an employee of Butcher's. Similarly, we cannot be certain of their exact date although they were probably made between the years 1893 (since the accompanying lecture refers to *Sir* John Tenniel, and it was in that year that the artist received his knighthood) and 1898 (when they were mentioned in Stuart Dodgson Collingwood's biography, *The Life and Letters of Lewis Carroll*).

As has been said, the pictures are based on Tenniel's illustrations, and some, such as Bill popping out of the chimney, or Alice with the giant Puppy, closely follow the originals. Others, however, contain small but fascinating differences. For example, Tenniel's first illustration of the White Rabbit shows him, with an umbrella under one arm, consulting a pocket-watch, whereas the first lantern slide shows the Rabbit, now carrying a walking stick, about to dive down the rabbit hole with Alice in pursuit.

Alice has also been added to other pictures: observing the Fish Footman delivering his invitation; and watching as the Hatter and the March Hare stuff the Dormouse into a teapot.

Several of the illustrations, including the White Rabbit in the cucumber frame and Alice talking to the Caterpillar, have been reversed, while others, such as the Duchess' kitchen and the scenes on the seashore have been completely reworked, with Alice looking far more lively than she does in Tenniel's drawings.

Some slides incorporate ideas from more than one of Tenniel's illustrations: among them the Hatter giving his evidence at the Trial; and the picture of the Pool of Tears, which now contains the birds from the Caucus Race. But, even more interesting are those depicting scenes Tenniel never drew, such as Alice finding the key on the glass table or growing "a mile high" in the courtroom.

The text which accompanies the pictures is that of the original Lantern Lecture, faithfully abridged from the published book and divided into three chapters: "Down the Rabbit Hole" (Slides 1-8), "The Mad Tea Party" (9-16) and "Who Stole the Tarts?" (17-24).

Try now to imagine that you are back in the year 1897, in the parlour of a large Victorian house. The heavy, velvet curtains are drawn against the night, a fire crackles on the hearth, the lamps are turned down low, and brightly-colored pictures appear and disappear on the wall—as if by magic. . . .

Brian Sibley

Alice was getting very tired of having nothing to do: the hot day made her feel sleepy and stupid, and too lazy even to make daisy-chains. Suddenly a White Rabbit, with pink eyes, ran close by her. There was nothing very remarkable in that, but it was rather odd to hear the Rabbit say to itself, "Oh dear! Oh dear! I shall be too late!" and when it actually took a watch out of its waistcoat pocket, looked at it and then hurried on, Alice started to her feet, and, burning with curiosity, ran across the field after it. It popped down a large rabbit-hole under the hedge, and in another moment down went Alice after it.

The rabbit-hole went straight on like a tunnel for some time, and then dipped suddenly down, so suddenly that before Alice could stop she found herself falling down a very deep well. Presently, thump! thump! down she came on a heap of dry leaves, and the fall was over. Alice jumped up, and found herself in a long, low hall; the Rabbit was no longer to be seen. There were doors all round the hall, but they were all locked, and Alice wondered how she was ever to get out again.

Suddenly she came upon a little glass table, and on it a tiny golden key. This key belonged to a little door which opened into a small passage, and beyond was the loveliest garden you ever saw. But how was poor Alice to get through? She went back to the table, and found on it a bottle with a label with the words, "DRINK ME." She tasted it, and finding it very nice, soon finished it. "What a curious feeling," said Alice, "I must be shutting up like a telescope." And so it was indeed; she was now only ten inches high, and could get through the little door into the lovely garden. But alas! the key was on the table and she could not reach it, nor could she climb up the slippery table leg, though she tried. So the poor little thing sat down and cried. Then she saw a glass box under the table: in it was a small cake with the words "EAT ME" marked in currants. So she soon finished off the cake.

"**C**uriouser and curiouser!" cried Alice, "now I'm opening out like the largest telescope that ever was! Goodbye, feet! Oh, my poor little feet! I wonder who will put on your shoes and stockings now for you dears? I'm sure I shan't be able! I shall be a great deal too far off to trouble myself about you; you must manage the best way you can — but I must be kind to them," thought Alice, "or perhaps they won't walk the way I want to go! Let me see; I'll give them a new pair of boots every Christmas. They must go by the carrier; how funny it'll seem sending presents to one's own feet! And how odd the directions will look: 'Alice's Right Foot, Esq., Hearthrug, near the Fender (with Alice's love). Oh dear, what nonsense I'm talking!"

Then her head struck against the roof of the hall, for she was now more than nine feet high. She had got the key, but to get into the garden was more hopeless than ever. She sat down and began to cry again, shedding gallons of tears, until there was a large pool all round her.

After a time she heard a pattering of feet in the distance. It was the White Rabbit, who dropped a fan and a pair of white gloves as he hurried past. She picked up the fan and began to fan herself as she thought over her troubles. But she discovered that she was shrinking rapidly: she found that the fan was the cause of this, and dropped it just in time to avoid shrinking away altogether. But the key was still on the table. "Things are worse than ever," thought poor Alice, "for I never was so small as this before, never! And I declare it's too bad, that it is!" As she said these words her foot slipped, and splash! she was up to her chin in salt water. She had fallen into the pool of tears which she had wept when she was nine feet high.

There was a mouse splashing about a little way off, which had slipped in like herself. "Would it be any use now to speak to this mouse?" thought Alice. "I'll try." So she began, "Oh, mouse, do you know the way out of this pool? I am very tired of swimming about here, oh mouse" – but the mouse only winked at her.

"Perhaps it doesn't understand English," she thought. "I daresay it's a French mouse, come over with William the Conqueror." So she tried it with the first sentence in her French lesson-book: "Où est ma chatte?" and the mouse gave a sudden leap out of the water and seemed to quiver all over with fright. "Oh, I beg your pardon," cried Alice, "I quite forgot that you didn't like cats!"

But in spite of all Alice's efforts her talk would return to the subject of cats and dogs, much to the poor mouse's disgust. Presently they swam to the shore with a number of other creatures who had fallen into the water – a dodo, a lory, an eaglet, an owl, and several others. They were all wet and cross and uncomfortable, so they ran about till they were all dry again, and then sat down in a ring to listen to the mouse's tale. But Alice again began talking about Dinah, her dear

old cat, and the subject was just as distasteful to the birds as to the mouse, so the party soon dispersed and Alice was left alone.

Then there was a pattering of little feet – it was the White Rabbit, looking for his fan and gloves. "Why, Mary Ann what *are* you doing out here?" said the Rabbit, "run home this moment, and fetch me a pair of gloves and a fan! Quick now!" Alice ran off, and soon found a neat little house, on the door of which was a bright brass plate with the name "W. RABBIT" engraved upon it. Here on a table she found the fan and gloves, and she also found another little bottle. She drank its contents, hoping that they would make her grow bigger, she was quite tired of being such a tiny little thing!

They did indeed: she grew and grew until she had to lie down on the floor with head pressed against the ceiling, one foot up the chimney and one arm out of the window. No wonder she felt unhappy. "It was much pleasanter at home," thought poor Alice, "when one wasn't always growing larger and smaller, and being ordered about by mice and rabbits." Presently the Rabbit came to look for her, but her elbow was pressed against the door and it could not get into the room. Alice heard it say to itself, "Then I'll go round and get in at the window."

"**T**hat you won't!" thought Alice, and after waiting till she heard the Rabbit just under the window, she suddenly spread out her hand, and made a snatch in the air. There was a shriek and a fall, and a crash of broken glass – the Rabbit had fallen into a cucumber frame or something of the sort.

Then came an angry voice – the Rabbit's – "Pat! Pat! where are you?" And then a voice she had not heard before, "Sure, then, I'm here! digging for apples, your honour!" "Digging for apples, indeed!" said the Rabbit angrily. "Here! come and help me out of *this*!" (Sounds of more broken glass.) "Now tell me, Pat, what's that in the window?" "Sure it's an arm, your honour!" "An arm, you goose, whoever saw one that size? Why, it fills the whole window." "Sure, it does, your honour; but it's an arm for all that." "Well, it's got no business there, at any rate; go and take it away!" But Pat seemed to think that was more easily said than done.

Presently Alice heard the rumbling of little cart-wheels, and a number of voices talking together. Then a ladder was raised to the roof, and someone named "Bill" was ordered by the Rabbit to go down the chimney. "Oh! so Bill's got to come down the chimney, has he?" said Alice to herself. "I wouldn't be in Bill's place for a good deal; this fireplace is narrow, to be sure, but I *think* I can kick a little!" She waited till she heard some little animal scrambling about in the chimney, and then gave one sharp kick.

"There goes Bill!" shouted a general chorus of voices, and the Rabbit called out "Catch him, you by the hedge! Hold up his head – brandy now – don't choke him!" When Bill was somewhat recovered, the Rabbit proposed to burn the house down. "If you do," Alice called out, "I'll set Dinah at you!" Then a shower of little pebbles came rattling in at the window, and turned into little cakes as they fell upon the floor. Alice ate one of these, and was delighted to find that she began shrinking directly. As soon as she was small enough to get through the door she ran out of the house and soon found herself safe in the shelter of a thick wood. As she peered about among the trees a little sharp bark just over her head made her look up in a great hurry.

An enormous puppy was looking down at her with large round eyes, and feebly stretching out one paw, trying to touch her. "Poor little thing!" said Alice, in a coaxing tone, but she was terribly afraid of it all the same. She picked up a little bit of stick and held it out to the Puppy, which ran at it with a yelp of delight, and made believe to worry it. Then Alice dodged behind a great thistle, to keep herself from being run over, and the moment she appeared on the other side, the Puppy made another rush at the stick.

Alice thought it was very much like having a game of play with a cart-horse, and was very glad when the Puppy got tired and sat down, panting, with its tongue hanging out of its mouth, and its great eyes half shut. She took this opportunity to escape, and set herself to consider how she was to become the right size again. "I suppose I ought to eat or drink something or other, but the great question is, what?"

There was a large mushroom growing near her, about the same height as herself, and on the top of it sat a large Caterpillar, quietly smoking a long hookah. "Who are *you*?" said the Caterpillar. "I hardly know, sir, just at present," said Alice; "at least I know who I *was* when I got up this morning, but I think I must have been changed several times since then – being so many different sizes in a day is very confusing." "It isn't," said the Caterpillar. "Well, perhaps you haven't found it so yet." said Alice; "but when you have to turn into a chrysalis, and after that into a butterfly, I should think you'll feel a little queer, won't you?" "Not a bit," said the Caterpillar, "Who are *you*?" which brought them back again to the beginning of the conversation.

Alice thought the Caterpillar was very contradictory and easily offended, and pointed out that it was very wretched to be only three inches high. The Caterpillar on the other hand declared that it was a very good height indeed – it was exactly three inches high itself.

At last it got down off the mushroom, and crawled away into the grass, remarking as it went, "One side of the mushroom will make you grow taller, the other side will make you grow shorter." As the mushroom was quite round it was not easy to decide which were the two sides: so Alice stretched her arms around it as far they would go, and broke off a bit of the edge with each hand. Then, nibbling first one bit and then the other, she at length succeeded in bringing herself to the height she desired, about nine inches.

Alice approached a little house standing in a clear place in the wood. She saw a footman with a fish's head just rapping at the door with his knuckles, and it was opened by another footman, who looked very much like a frog. The Fish-Footman handed a very large letter to the other, saying, "For the Duchess. An invitation from the Queen to play croquet." Then they both bowed low, and their curls got entangled together, which made Alice laugh so much that she had to run back into the wood for fear of their hearing her. When she next peeped out the Fish-Footman was gone, and the other was sitting on the ground near the door, staring stupidly up into the sky. Alice knocked at the door, then opened it and went in.

The door led into a large kitchen, full of smoke from one end to the other: the Duchess was sitting on a three-legged stool in the middle nursing a baby; the Cook was leaning over the fire stirring a large cauldron, which seemed to be full of soup. "There's certainly too much pepper in that soup!" Alice said to herself, as well as she could for sneezing. There was certainly too much in the air. The Duchess sneezed: the baby sneezed and howled alternately. Indeed, the only things in the kitchen that did not sneeze were the Cook and the Cat.

"Please would you tell me," asked Alice, "Why your cat grins like that?" "It's a Cheshire Cat," said the Duchess, "and that's why." And now the Cook took the cauldron of soup off the fire, and at once began to throw everything within her reach at the Duchess and the baby: the fire-irons came first, then followed a shower of saucepans, plates and dishes. The Duchess took no notice of them even when they hit her, and the baby was howling so much already, that it was quite impossible to say whether the blows hurt it or not. "Here, you may nurse it a bit, if you like!" the Duchess said to Alice, flinging the baby at her, "I must get ready to play croquet with the Queen."

Alice caught the baby with some difficulty: it was a queer shaped little creature, and held out its arms and legs in all directions, "just like a star fish," thought Alice. As she carried it out into the open air it left off sneezing and began to grunt. "Don't grunt," said Alice, "that's not at all a proper way of expressing yourself." But the baby grunted again. "If you're going to turn into a pig, my dear," said Alice seriously, "I'll have nothing more to do with you. Mind now!" Another grunt, and she looked down into its face in some alarm: there could be no mistake about it, it was neither more nor less than a pig, and she felt that it would be quite absurd to carry it any further. So she set it down, and it trotted quietly away into the wood. "If it had grown up," she said to herself, "it would have made a dreadfully ugly child, but it makes rather a handsome pig, I think."

And now she saw the Cheshire Cat sitting on the boughs of a tree a few yards off. "Cheshire Puss," said Alice respectfully – and the Cat grinned more than ever – "would you tell me, please, which way I ought to go from here?" "In that direction, the Cat said, waving its paw round, "lives a Hatter, and in *that* direction," waving the other paw, "lives a March Hare. Visit either you like, they're both mad." Then it vanished re-appearing again to ask, "What became of the baby?" "It turned into a pig," said Alice. "I thought it would," said the Cat, and vanished again. Alice decided to visit the March Hare. "I've seen Hatters before," she thought to herself, "and perhaps as this is May the Hare won't be raving mad – at least not so mad as it was in March."

As she walked on the Cat appeared again, sitting on the branch of a tree. "Did you say pig or fig?" said the Cat. "I said pig," replied Alice, "and I wish you wouldn't keep appearing and vanishing so suddenly, you make one quite giddy." "All right," said the Cat, and this time it vanished quite slowly, beginning with the end of the tail, and ending with the grin, which remained some time after the rest of it had gone. "Well, I've often seen a cat without a grin," thought Alice, "but a grin without a cat! It's the most curious thing I ever saw in all my life!"

The house of the March Hare now came in sight: the chimneys were shaped like ears, and the roof was thatched with fur. As it was rather large, Alice nibbled a bit of the mushroom and raised herself to a height of two feet before approaching it.

There was a table set out under a tree in front of the house, and the March Hare and the Hatter were having tea at it; a Dormouse was sitting between them, fast asleep. The table was a large one, but the three were all crowded together at one corner of it. "No room! no room!" they cried out when they saw Alice coming.

"There's *plenty* of room," said Alice, and sat down in a large arm-chair at one end of the table. "Have some wine," the March Hare said, in an encouraging tone. Alice could not see any wine on the table and said so. "There isn't any," said the March Hare. "Then it wasn't very civil of you to offer it," said Alice, angrily.

"Your hair wants cutting," said the Hatter, who had been looking at Alice with great curiosity. "You shouldn't make personal remarks," Alice said, with some severity; "it's very rude." The Hatter opened his eyes very wide on hearing this; but all he said was, "Why is a raven like a writing-desk?" "Come, we shall have some fun now!" thought Alice, "I'm glad they've begun asking riddles" – and she sat silently thinking over all she could remember about ravens and writing-desks, which wasn't much.

The Hatter had taken his watch out of his pocket, and was looking at it uneasily, shaking it every now and then, and holding it to his ear. "I told you butter wouldn't suit the works," he said, looking angrily at the March Hare. "It was the *best* butter," the March Hare meekly replied. "Yes, but some crumbs *must* have got in as well," the Hatter grumbled: "you shouldn't have put it in with the bread-knife." The March Hare took the watch and looked at it gloomily: then he dipped it into his cup of tea and looked at it again: but he could think of nothing better to say than his first remark, "It was the *best* butter, you know."

The Hatter changed the subject by remarking, "The Dormouse is asleep again," and he poured a little hot tea upon its nose. The Dormouse shook its head impatiently, and said, without opening its eyes, "Of course, of course; just what I was going to remark myself."

"Have you guessed the riddle yet?" the Hatter said, turning to Alice. "No, I give it up," Alice replied; "what's the answer?" "I haven't the slightest idea," said the Hatter. "Nor I," said the March Hare. Alice sighed wearily. "I think you might do something better with the time," she said, "than waste it asking riddles with no answers."

The March Hare now proposed that the Dormouse should tell a story. "Wake up, Dormouse!" And they pinched it on both sides at once. The Dormouse slowly opened his eyes. "Tell us a story!" said the March Hare. "Yes, please do!" pleaded Alice. "Once upon a time there were three little sisters," the Dormouse began: "and their names were Elsie, Lacie, and Tillie; and they lived at the bottom of a well –" "What did they live on?" asked Alice. "Treacle," said the Dormouse: "It was a treacle well." "Why, there's no such thing," said Alice, but the Hatter and the March Hare went "Sh! Sh!" and the Dormouse proceeded.

"And so these three little sisters – they were learning to draw, you know–" "What did they draw?" said Alice. "Treacle," said the Dormouse. "But where did they draw the treacle from?" asked Alice. "You can draw water out of a water-well," said the Hatter; "so I should think you could draw treacle out of a treacle-well, – eh, stupid?" "But they were *in* the well," said Alice. "Of course they were, – well in. They were learning to draw," the Dormouse proceeded, "and they drew all manner of things – everything that begins with

an M, such as mouse-traps, and the moon, and memory, and muchness – you know you say things are 'much of a muchness' – did you ever see such a thing as a drawing of a muchness!" "Really, now you ask me," said Alice, very much confused, "I don't think–" "Then you shouldn't talk," said the Hatter. This piece of rudeness was more than Alice could bear; she got up in great disgust, and walked off.

As she looked back, she saw them trying to put the Dormouse into the teapot. "At any rate, I'll never go there again!" said Alice; "It's the stupidest tea-party I ever was at in all my life!" And now she noticed that one of the trees had a door leading right into it. Through she went, and found herself again in the long hall, and close to the little glass table. She took the key and unlocked the door that led into the garden.

Then she made herself a foot high, walked down the little passage, and found herself at last in the beautiful garden, among the bright flower-beds and the cool fountains.

A large rose-tree stood near the entrance of the garden: the roses growing on it were white, but there were three gardeners at it, busily painting them red. "Would you tell me," said Alice, "why you are painting those roses?" One of the gardeners answered: "Why, the fact is, you see, Miss, this here ought to have been a *red* rose-tree, and we put a white one in by mistake; and if the Queen was to find it out, we should all have our heads cut off, you know. So you see, Miss, we're doing our best afore she comes, to –" At this moment, Five called out, "The Queen! The Queen!" and the three gardeners threw themselves flat upon the ground.

Alice turned to find herself face to face with the Queen of Hearts. "Who is this?" said the Queen; "What's your name, child?" "My name is Alice, so please your Majesty," said Alice, very politely; but she added, to herself, "Why, they're only a pack of cards, after all. I needn't be afraid of them!"

"Off with their heads!" cried the Queen, when she found out what the three gardeners had been doing, but Alice saved them by putting them into a large flower-pot that stood near, and where the soldiers could not see them. "Can you play croquet?" the Queen asked Alice. Alice replied, "Yes." "Come on, then," said the Queen, and the procession moved on to the croquet ground. It was the most curious game that Alice had ever played: the ground was all ridges and furrows, the balls were live hedge-hogs, the mallets live flamingoes, and the soldiers doubled themselves up and stood upon their hands and feet to make the arches.

Alice found a great difficulty in managing her flamingo: it would twist itself round and look up in her face, with such a puzzled expression, that she could not help laughing, whilst the hedge-hogs crawled away just when she wanted to hit them, and the doubled-up soldiers were always getting up and walking off to other parts of the ground. It was a very difficult game indeed.

Presently she noticed a curious appearance in the air. It puzzled her at first, but soon she made it out to be a grin, and she said to herself, "It's the Cheshire Cat: now I shall have somebody to talk to."

Only the Cat's head appeared: it seemed to think that was sufficient. "Who *are* you talking to?" said the King, coming up to Alice. "It's a friend of mine – a Cheshire Cat," said Alice, "allow me to introduce it." "I don't like the look of it at all," said the King, "it must be removed," and he called to the Queen, "My dear! I wish you would have this Cat removed!" "Off with his head!" answered the Queen. But here a difficulty arose, and the question was hotly argued. The executioner said that you couldn't cut off a head unless there was a body to cut it off from; the King said that anything that had a head could be beheaded; and the Queen said that if something wasn't done about it in less than no time, she'd have everybody executed all round. The Cat settled the question by quietly fading away, and the players went back to their game.

Presently the Queen asked Alice, "Have you seen the Mock Turtle yet?" "No" said Alice, "I don't even know what a Mock Turtle is." "It's a thing that Mock Turtle Soup is made from," said the Queen; "Come on and he shall tell you his history."

Very soon they came upon a Gryphon, and the Queen put Alice in his charge, saying she had to go back and see after some executions. "What fun!" said the Gryphon. "What *is* the fun?" said Alice. "Why, *she*," said the Gryphon. "It's all her fancy, that: they never executes nobody, you know. Come on!" So they came to the Mock Turtle, sitting sad and lonely on a ledge of rock, and sighing as if his heart would break. "This here young lady", said the Gryphon, "she wants for to know your history, she do."

With many sobs and eyes full of tears, the Mock Turtle told his story. "Once," he began, "I was a real Turtle. When we were little we went to school in the sea. The master was an old Turtle: we used to call him Tortoise." "Why did you call him Tortoise, if he wasn't one?" Alice asked. "We called him Tortoise because he taught us. We had the best of educations. I took the regular course – couldn't afford extras. There was Reeling and Writhing to begin with, and then the different branches of Arithmetic: Ambition, Distraction, Uglification and Derision. Never heard of Uglification? You know what to beautify is, I suppose?" "Yes," said Alice, "it means to make anything prettier." "Well, then, if you don't know what to uglify is you must be a simpleton."

"What else had you to learn?" asked Alice. "Well, there was Mystery, ancient and modern, with Seaography, then Drawling: the Drawling Master was an old Conger Eel, that used to come once a week; he taught us Drawling, Sketching and Fainting in Coils." "Tell her about the games," said the Gryphon. The Mock Turtle sighed deeply, and with difficulty repressed his sobs. "You may not have lived much under the sea," he went on, "and perhaps were never even introduced to a Lobster, so you can have no idea what a delightful thing a Lobster Quadrille is."

"No, indeed," said Alice. "What sort of a dance is it?" "Why" said the Gryphon, "you first form into a line along the sea shore." "Two lines!" cried the Mock Turtle, "Seals, Turtles and so on, then, when you've cleared the jelly-fish out of the way, you advance twice."

"Each with a Lobster as a partner," cried the Gryphon. "Of course," the Mock Turtle said. "Advance twice, set to partners, change Lobsters, and retire in same order," continued the Gryphon. "Then, you know," the Mock Turtle went on, "you throw the—" "The Lobsters!" shouted the Gryphon, with a bound into the air– "as far out to sea as you can–" "Swim after them," screamed the Gryphon. "Turn a somersault in the sea," cried the Mock Turtle, capering wildly about. "Change Lobsters again," yelled the Gryphon. "Back to land again and that's all the first figure," said the Mock Turtle. "Would you like to see a little of it?" "Very much, indeed," said Alice. So they began solemnly dancing round and round Alice, singing as they went, and waving their fore paws to mark the time. Then they had more talk, and a song about "Turtle Soup," which was interrupted by a cry in the distance.

"The trial's beginning!" The King and Queen were seated on their throne when they arrived, with a great crowd assembled about them: all sorts of little birds and beasts, as well as the whole pack of cards. The Knave was standing before them in chains, and near the King was the White Rabbit. In the middle of the court was a table, with a large dish of tarts upon it, and in the jury-box were twelve "creatures," as Alice called them, for some of them were animals and some birds; they all had slates, and one of them (it was poor little Bill, the lizard) had a pencil that squeaked, so Alice took it away from him. "Herald, read the accusation," said the King, and the White Rabbit read from his scroll: "The Queen of Hearts, she made some tarts, all on a summer's day; the Knave of Hearts, he stole those tarts, and took them quite away!"

"Consider your verdict," the King said to the Jury. "Not yet, not yet!" the Rabbit hastily interrupted, "there's a great deal to come before that!" "Then call the first witness," said the King.

The first witness was the Hatter. He came in with a teacup in one hand a piece of bread-and-butter in the other, for he hadn't quite finished his tea when he was sent for. "You ought to have finished," said the King; "When did you begin?" "14th of March, I think it was," he said. "15th," said the March Hare. "16th," said the Dormouse. "Write that down," the King said to the Jury, and the Jury wrote all three dates down on their slates, and then added them up, and reduced the answer to shillings and pence. "Take off your hat," the King said. "It isn't mine," said the Hatter. "*Stolen!*" the King exclaimed. "I keep them to sell," the Hatter added, "I've none of my own." "Give your evidence," said the King, "and don't be nervous, or I'll have you executed on the spot."

But the Hatter *was* nervous, and in his confusion bit a large piece out of his teacup instead of the bread-and-butter. "I'm a poor man, your Majesty," he began in a trembling voice, "and I hadn't begun my tea – not above a week or so – and what with the

bread-and-butter getting so thin – and the twinkling of the tea–" "The twinkling of *what*?" said the King. "It began with the tea," the Hatter replied. "Of course twinkling begins with a T," said the King sharply. "Do you take me for a dunce? Go on." "I'm a poor man," the Hatter went on, "and most things twinkled after that – so I can't remember–" "You must remember," remarked the King, "or I'll have you executed."

The miserable Hatter dropped his teacup and bread-and-butter, and went down on one knee. "I'm a poor man, your Majesty," he began. "You're a *very* poor *speaker*," said the King, "and if that's all you know about it, you may stand down." So the Hatter hurriedly left the court.

The next witness was the Duchess's Cook, who brought her pepper-box, and set everyone sneezing. "Give your evidence," said the King. "Shan't," said the Cook, so they didn't get anything out of her.

Alice for some time had been feeling a very curious sensation, which puzzled her a good deal until she made out what it was – she was growing larger again. Quite forgetting this in her surprise at hearing the White Rabbit call on "Alice" as next witness, she jumped up and tipped over the jury-box with the edge of her skirt, upsetting all the Jurymen on the heads of the crowd below, and there they lay sprawling about, reminding her very much of a globe of gold-fish she had accidentally upset the week before. "Oh, I *beg* your pardon!" she exclaimed in a tone of great dismay, and began picking them up again as quickly as she could. "The trial cannot proceed until all the Jurymen are back in their proper places," said the King. Alice found she had put the Lizard in head downwards, but she soon put that right.

"What do you know about this business?" the King said to Alice. "Nothing," said Alice. Then the King, who had been busily writing in his notebook, called out "Silence!" and read from his book, "Rule 42. *All persons more than a mile high to leave the court.*" Everybody looked at Alice. "*I'm* not a mile high," said Alice. "You are," said the King. "Nearly two miles high," added the Queen. "Well, I shan't go, at any rate," said Alice. "Besides that's not a regular rule, you invented it just now." "It's the oldest rule in the book," said the King. "Then it ought to be Number One," said Alice.

Again the King turned to the Jury: "Consider your verdict," he said. "No, no!" said the Queen, "sentence first, verdict afterwards." "Stuff and nonsense!" said Alice loudly. "Off with her head!" shouted the Queen. "Who cares for you," said Alice, "you're nothing but a pack of cards!"

And then the whole pack rose up into the air, and came flying down upon her. She gave a little scream and tried to beat them off, and then found herself lying on the bank with her head in her sister's lap, whilst some dead leaves fluttered down from the trees upon her face. "Oh, I've had such a curious dream!" said Alice, and she told her sister of her strange adventures in Wonderland.

ACKNOWLEDGEMENTS

The author and the publisher gratefully acknowledge
the kind assistance of Lester Smith and Dr Andrew Brown of
the Cambridge University, and, in particular, thank Denis Crutch
for kindly loaning four lantern slides for reproduction.